For Violet Carman Rigg—YP

For Jade and Zoe who already love
the garden—DM

Scholastic Australia
345 Pacific Highway Lindfield NSW 2070
An imprint of Scholastic Australia Pty Limited
PO Box 579 Gosford NSW 2250
ABN 11 000 614 577
www.scholastic.com.au

Part of the Scholastic Group
Sydney · Auckland · New York · Toronto · London · Mexico City
· New Delhi · Hong Kong · Buenos Aires · Puerto Rico

Published by Scholastic Australia in 2014.
Text and illustrations copyright © Scholastic Australia, 2014.
Text by Yvette Poshoglian.
Cover design, illustrations and inside illustrations by Danielle McDonald.

National Library of Australia Cataloguing-in-Publication entry

Author: Poshoglian, Yvette, author.
Title: Flower power / Yvette Poshoglian; illustrated by Danielle McDonald.
ISBN: 9781743620533 (paperback)
Series: Poshoglian, Yvette. Ella and Olivia; 11.
Target Audience: For primary school age.
Subjects: Gardening--Juvenile fiction.
Gardens--Juvenile fiction.
Sisters--Juvenile fiction.
Other Authors/Contributors: McDonald, Danielle, illustrator.
Dewey Number: A823.4

Typeset in Buccardi.

Printed by McPherson's Printing Group, Maryborough, VIC.

Scholastic Australia's policy, in association with McPherson's Printing Group, is to use
papers that are renewable and made efficiently from wood grown in responsibly managed forests,
so as to minimise its environmental footprint.

10 9 8 7 6 5 4   15 16 17 18 / 1

By
Yvette Poshoglian

Illustrated by
Danielle McDonald

A Scholastic Australia Book

Chapter One

Ella and Olivia are sisters.
Ella is seven years old.
Olivia is five-and-a-half
years old. Ella loves being
the BIG sister. She also loves
to draw and dance. Olivia
is learning to play netball.
She loves collecting Cool
Kitties. The girls have the
same shade of brown hair.
They both have freckles.

Ella and Olivia have a little brother called Max and, of course, there is Bob, their puppy. Bob has thick golden fur that seems to get everywhere.

Ella has a plan. A big, **GREEN** plan! She wants to create a special garden in the backyard. There is a lot of work ahead.

Olivia also wants to help with the garden. But Ella wants to be in charge of everything!

The backyard is very messy, thanks to their puppy, Bob. Bob loves to dig and scratch and sniff. Right now, he thinks everyone wants to play with him. He wags his tail. He sniffs the air. Then he gives a little woof. Bob is very happy.

The girls are very excited about their big, green plan.

Ella and Olivia are learning about gardens at school. All the classes take it in turns to look after the vegie patch. Each grade has a different part of the garden to look after.

Ella has made a list of all the things she needs to do for her new backyard garden:

Measure up the garden

Dig the soil

Plant the vegies

Water the plants

Ella wants to grow lots of
different types of vegies
in the new garden. Olivia
wants to grow flowers.

'What about string beans,
tomatoes and chives?'
Mum says.
'Or daisies, peonies and
marigolds?' says Dad.
'No way, Dad,' says Ella,
shaking her head. 'It's
going to be a vegie patch.'

'I want to grow flowers!'
says Olivia.
But Ella doesn't listen.
'You'll have real green
thumbs,' Mum says.
'Green what?' Olivia asks.
'When someone loves to
grow things in the garden
you say they have green
thumbs,' Mum explains.
'That's us!' Olivia cries.
Max sings in agreement.
But Ella doesn't say
anything.

Ella wants her garden to be just like the herb and vegetable garden at school.

'We are growing chives, dill and coriander in our part of the garden,' says Ella.

'What's that?' Olivia asks.

'Coriander smells very fresh,' says Ella.

'Chives are long and skinny,' says Mum. 'They taste a bit like onions. But they don't make you cry when you cut them.'

'So I don't have to wear my goggles?' Dad asks. He uses his swimming goggles in the pool and in the kitchen!

Olivia wants to choose flowers for the new garden. Nanna and Grandad have a beautiful garden full of tropical flowers. They have hibiscus and frangipani plants. They have tall, green palm trees.

Olivia wants to grow
flowers in bright colours—
purples, pinks and oranges.

Mum and Dad will help
the girls build the garden.
Then Ella and Olivia will
be in charge of planting,
growing and watering.
'You can't forget to water
the garden,' Dad warns.
'Everything will shrivel up
and die if you don't look
after it.'

But Ella thinks it's HER garden!

'I will do it all, Dad. It's MY vegie patch,' says Ella.

'I'm sure there'll be enough room in the garden for everyone to grow what they like, Ella,' Mum says.

But Olivia stomps off inside the house. Why does Ella have to be so bossy?

Chapter Two

The weekend finally arrives. Saturday is gardening day! Ella and Olivia leap out of bed. Ella pulls on her jeans and her gumboots. Olivia puts on her overalls and boots, too. Things can get very dirty and messy in the garden. 'We can't forget our hats,' says Ella.

Ella has a straw hat with a purple ribbon around it. Olivia's hat has a pink ribbon around it.

Mum and Dad are already busy in the backyard. Max is making mud pies. Dad wears his gardening hat. Mum *squelches* in her gumboots.

Dad measures up the garden and puts some stakes in the ground. Mum saws some timber that will form the edge of the garden. Bob runs around and around in excitement.

21

'Mum and Dad are a good team,' says Ella.
'So are we!' says Olivia.
But Ella doesn't say anything.

'There are presents for you girls on the table,' Mum calls out. 'They are from Nanna and Grandad.'
Ella and Olivia squeal with delight. They love presents! They run to the table and tear open the bag.

Inside are two sets of gardening gloves. Ella's gloves are purple. Olivia's gloves are pink. And they fit . . . just like gloves. Gardening gloves will protect their hands when digging in the dirt. Now the girls are perfectly dressed for a day in the garden.

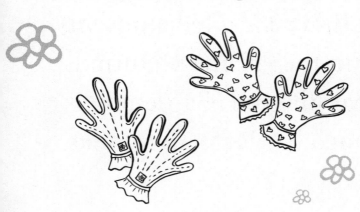

Ella and Olivia are ready to get to work in the backyard.

'Phew,' says Dad. He is very sweaty from digging a big patch of the garden. He hands the shovel to Ella. 'Your turn,' he says.

Ella picks up the shovel. It is HEAVY! She pushes it in the ground to turn over the soil. Gardening is much harder than it looks.

'Come and help me, Olivia,' says Mum. Together, they lay the pieces of timber between the stakes. These will be the edges of the garden.

A few hours later, Ella and Olivia are nearly done. Ella and Dad dug up the garden. New soil is laid over the top.

Mum and Olivia's timber edge around the patch is finished. Hopefully it will keep Bob out.

Bob sniffs every corner. He buries his nose in the soil. He leaps up and starts to dig a hole in the new garden.

'**NO, BOB!**' everyone yells together. Bob stops and jumps out of the garden.

'That was close,' says Ella.
'Too close,' says Olivia.
'We'll have to keep an eye on Bob,' she says.
'Maybe with the hose?' Dad suggests.
'No, Dad!' the girls say together.

Gardening is hard work.
Ella's and Olivia's hands
are sore. It's lucky they
were wearing their new
gloves. That night, as they
go to bed, they look at
their hands. They are red.

'It will be worth it,' says Ella.
'I can't wait to plant the flowers,' says Olivia.
Tonight the new garden is just a patch. By this time tomorrow, it will be a vegie patch, Ella thinks.

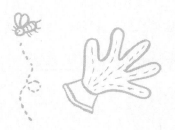

Chapter Three

Ella is the first to wake up the next morning. Her legs and arms ache! All that digging with the shovel has made her sore all over.

Olivia is still snoring in bed. Ella runs out to check on the garden. She can see Bob is still fast asleep in his doghouse.

Ella is excited about her garden. She checks her new list.

Plant vegie seeds

Choose herbs

no FLOWERS!

31

This garden has to be just like the one at school. Ella doesn't want any flowers getting in the way. Ella just wants to grow things you can eat and use. It will be a bit like having a farm in the city.

That morning, the girls go to the nursery with Mum and Dad. A nursery sells plants, flowers, seeds and everything you need for a garden.

There are lots of people, young and old, buying plants. Sausages and onions are frying somewhere nearby.

'You girls are lucky to have such a big garden,' Mum says. 'Some people grow their plants in pots on their balconies.'
'My vegie patch is going to be HUGE!' says Ella.

There are hundreds of types of plants and flowers at the nursery. Ella chooses her cucumber, bean and chive seeds. Olivia chooses her flower seeds. She likes purple flowers like pansies and violets.

Mum puts some seedlings and tomato plants in the trolley.

'Where's Dad?' Mum asks.

They find Dad and Max
at the front of the nursery
at the sausage sizzle.
'Max and I needed some
energy,' Dad says.

'Hurry up!' says Ella. 'We have to go home and plant everything now!'
Mum and Dad sigh. Ella can be so bossy sometimes.

The girls prepare the garden with their new treasures. Ella and Mum plant the string beans and the tomatoes. The tomatoes will grow up a wooden stake planted next to each seedling.

Olivia and Dad help plant
the vegetable and herb
seeds.

Soon the garden bed is
filled with rows and rows
of plants and seeds.
'Where are the flowers
going to go?' asks Olivia.
'We're not having flowers,'
says Ella. 'There's no room
now, anyway.'

Olivia is very disappointed, but she tries not to show it.

'Plants need a lot of water and sun to grow,' says Dad. 'You will need to make sure that you water the seeds and seedlings often.'

'I will water my vegie patch EVERY DAY,' says Ella.

'What about me?' asks Olivia. After all this hard work, she didn't even get to plant her flower seeds.

Mum finds two plant pots
in the shed.

'Here you go, Olivia,' she
says. 'You could plant some
of your flower seeds in
these for now.'

'Girls, you have to learn
to cooperate,' says Dad.
'Ella, you have been in
charge of the planting.
Now, it's Olivia's turn to be
responsible. She will take
care of the watering. Right,
Olivia?'

Both girls nod. But Olivia is very cross. She doesn't want anything more to do with the garden. In fact, she plans never to set foot in it again!

Chapter Four

All week long, Olivia
ignores the new garden.
Ella was so mean and bossy.
Instead, Olivia finds other
things to do. She takes
Bob for lots of walks. She
cleans her bookshelf. Olivia
practises her dancing in
front of the mirror. But she
does **NOT** water the vegie
patch.

Every day, Ella checks the garden. The seeds have not shot up yet. The seedlings stay the same size. In fact, they look thirsty!

'Be patient,' says Mum. 'That's the first rule of gardening.'

Ella is very *imp*atient. She wants to see her plants grow straight away.

At school, the garden is bigger and brighter than ever. Mr White has been showing the students how to pick the beans off the vine. Olivia's class picks tomatoes straight off the vine, and even get to taste some! Mr White hoses down the thirsty garden.

With so many living things growing, a garden needs plenty of water and sunlight to survive.

Two weeks go by. Ella waits and watches her vegie patch in the backyard. But the more she watches the soil and the seedlings, the less things seem to grow. 'A watched pot never boils,' says Mum finally.

Everything looks very dry. Some of the leaves are curling up and turning brown. The soil looks grey and hard, not dark and soft. 'Olivia, are you SURE you're watering the garden?' Ella begs. Olivia doesn't answer. She pretends not to hear.

'Olivia, when did you last give the vegie patch a drink?' asks Mum. But Olivia doesn't say anything.

The next day, Ella carefully inspects the tomatoes. She is sure they are not growing at all. Not even an extra millimetre! She is puzzled. Ella bends down to look closer. The leaves crumble under her touch. The tomato plants are bone dry.

She puts her finger in the soil. The soil is also dry. Nothing at all is growing in her garden. This is a gardening disaster! 'Olivia!' Ella cries, storming back inside. 'You're in **BIG** trouble!'

Chapter Five

Ella is furious. Olivia is angry. When both sisters get this angry, you never know what will happen next.

'You let the garden die!' says Ella. She holds some of the tomato leaves in her hand. They crumble into dust in front of Olivia.

'You were so bossy!' says Olivia. 'It's not my fault!'

'Yes, it is!' cries Ella.

'Mmrrphhhhhh!' says Max.

'BE QUIET, MAX!' Ella and
Olivia say together.

Max stops talking. He looks like he might cry. Suddenly the girls feel awful. Ella feels terrible about being bossy. Olivia feels terrible for letting the garden die.

'I'm sorry I was bossy!' Ella says.

'I'm sorry I didn't water the vegie patch,' says Olivia.

Then they both look at Max.
'SORRY, MAX!' they cry.
Ella and Olivia smother him
in kisses and cuddles.
'Maybe you should start
again, working together,'
says Dad.

'Why don't we go and have a look at the garden and see what we can save?'

Dad grabs his gardening hat from the hook on the back door. Ella pulls hers off the hook too. Then, because Olivia is shorter, Ella pulls hers down for her. Bob scampers out with them, followed by Max. Together, they all inspect the plants.

Dad touches the soil with his fingers. 'Very dry,' he says. He feels the leaves. They are crunchy and brown, instead of healthy and green.

Olivia feels terrible inside. It's such a waste. Ella looks at the empty rows in the vegie patch where the seeds should have grown. 'We need more plants here,' she says to Olivia.

'Maybe we could plant some pretty flowers?'

'Really?' says Olivia. 'I still have the seeds.' Olivia runs to the shed to get the seeds for the flower garden.

'Good idea, girls,' says Dad. 'Flowers attract bees and butterflies to the garden, too. They will help all the plants grow.'

56

That afternoon, the girls
dig up the dead part of
the vegie patch. Then they
divide the patch in two.
Together, they turn the soil
again. Ella hands Olivia the
shovel. Olivia can hardly
use it!

'It's too heavy,' Olivia says.

'I'll do it for you,' says Ella.
They work as a team to get
the garden ready all over
again.

Ella can see that there is plenty of room for both of them in the garden. Olivia feels a bit bad that the vegie patch died. She will water the new vegie patch properly this time!

Ella plants some more vegies and herbs. She feels terrible for bossing Olivia around. Maybe the flowers will be good in the garden . . .

Olivia plants her flower seeds.

'What are you growing, Olivia?' asks Ella.

'Sweet peas and pansies!' Olivia says.

Olivia is very neat when she plants her seeds. There needs to be space between the seeds so that they can grow properly.

'Mine are a bit messy,' says Ella. So Olivia helps Ella plant her chives and dill all over again.

After every last seed has been planted, Dad pulls the hose out and turns the tap on.

'You girls need to be very responsible from now on.' Both girls nod. 'No more fighting,' he says.

'We promise!' Ella and Olivia say together.

'Woof! Woof!' says Bob. Max claps his hands. Dad hands Ella and Olivia the hose.

'Make sure you give the vegie patch a good drink,' he says.

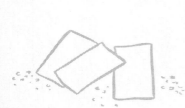

'It's not just a vegie patch, Dad,' says Ella. 'It's **OUR** garden.'

Ella takes the hose and Olivia takes the nozzle. And they water their flower and vegetable garden together.

COLLECT THEM ALL!

Cupcake Catastrophe

Best Friend Showdown

Ballet Stars

The New Girl

Puppy Trouble

The Big Sleepover

Pony Problem

Cool Kitties

The Christmas Surprise

Sports Carnival

Flower Power

Christmas Wonderland

Beach Holiday

Spelling Superstar

Hair Disaster

Friends Forever Stories

Super Sweet Stories

To find out more go to:
EllaandOlivia.com.au
where you can play games and do more
fun stuff!